Read all the Ninja Meerkats adventures!

The Clan of the Scorpion (#1)

The Eye of the Monkey (#2)

Escape from Ice Mountain (#3)

Hollywood Showdown (#4)

The Tomb of Doom (#5)

Big City Bust-Up (#6)

The Ultimate Dragon Warrior (#7)

Outback Attack (#8)

NINJA MEERKATS

OUTBACK ATTACK

GARETH P. JONES

SQUARE
FISH

NEW YORK

SQUARE
FISH

An Imprint of Macmillan
175 Fifth Avenue
New York, NY 10010
mackids.com

Square Fish books may be purchased for business or promotional use.
For information on bulk purchases, please contact the Macmillan Corporate
and Premium Sales Department at (800) 221-7945 x5442
or by e-mail at specialmarkets@macmillan.com.

Library of Congress Cataloging-in-Publication Data Available
ISBN 978-1-250-04667-3 (paperback) / ISBN 978-1-250-04943-8 (e-book)

Originally published in Great Britain by Stripes Publishing
First Square Fish Edition: 2014
Square Fish logo designed by Filomena Tuosto

10 9 8 7 6 5 4 3 2 1

**For the Aussie Whittakers,
Charlotte and Billy
~ G.P.J.**

Oh, you're here already. Sorry if I'm a bit late. You see, I'm rather slow these days. Recently I bought a walking stick to help me get about, but I'm afraid to say that it was hopeless. It refused to walk anywhere. It just stood there in the corner of the room. Between you and me, I think it was just an ordinary stick.

Next, I purchased some dancing shoes, but it was the same story. They didn't dance at all. Perhaps they didn't like the music I put on. But they should have danced. It was soul music after all. Or should that be *sole* music?

Anyway, four meerkats who have no difficulty getting around are the Clan of the Scorpion. They have dedicated many years to defending the world from the villainous Ringmaster and his evil circus troupe. They are . . .

Jet Flashfeet: a super-fast ninja whose only fault is craving the glory he so richly deserves.

Bruce "the muscle" Willowhammer: the strongest of the gang, though in the brain race he lags somewhat behind.

Donnie Dragonjab: a brilliant mind, inventor, and master of gadgets.

Chuck Cobracrusher: his clear leadership has saved the others' skins more times than I care to remember.

Oh, and me, Grandmaster One-Eye: as old and wise as the sand dunes themselves.

You may recall that the Clan finally defeated the Ringmaster, when he fell into a volcano on Dragon Island. Or did he?

I'm afraid I have no idea. I do know that this adventure takes place in Australia. So here's a poem by possum poet, Mel Bourne.

You can teach a kangaroo
To count to twenty-two,
You can teach a wallaby
To minus one from three.
All marsupials make excellent pupils,
They make even better school friends.
And their pouches come in quite handy
For keeping your pencils and pens.

Anyway, I'm off to see whether I can buy a flying jacket. I hope you enjoy this story . . . **OUTBACK ATTACK.**

CHAPTER ONE

BELLA WILLOWHAMMER

Bathed in the warm glow of the morning sun, the world-famous Sydney Opera House looked like it was made out of segments of a gigantic orange. Hidden between two of those segments were four ninja meerkats.

Donnie Dragonjab put away the grappling hook they had used to climb up there. "I wonder why your sister chose this as a meeting point, Bruce," he said.

"Search me," said Bruce. "But she definitely said in her e-mail to meet on the roof of the Opera House."

"I expect Bella chose it because it is discreet and yet easy to find for first-time visitors to Sydney," said Chuck.

"Who's this Sydney you keep talking about?" asked Bruce.

"Sydney is the name of the city, Bruce," said Jet.

"Oh yeah," replied Bruce, scratching his head.

"I'm amazed a sister of yours even knows how to send an e-mail," said Donnie. "The last time you tried to use the computer, you smashed it to pieces."

"You were the one who told me to boot it," protested Bruce.

"I said *re*boot it," replied Donnie.

"Yeah, well, Bella was always the smart Willowhammer," admitted Bruce.

"What does she do here in Australia?" asked Chuck.

"I don't know."

"I hope it's something exciting," said Jet. "Life's been so boring since we defeated our enemy, the Ringmaster."

"As followers of the Way of the Scorpion, we should not seek excitement and adventure," said Chuck.

"Yeah, but since he's gone, the closest we've had to some action was when Bruce thought that someone had stolen his packet of pickled newts' knees."

"It didn't take long to solve that one, did it, Bruce?" said Donnie pointedly.

"I told you, I forgot I ate them," said Bruce.

"The point is that since Chuck pushed the Ringmaster into the volcano on Dragon Island, everything has been as dull as dishwater," complained Jet.

"Now Jet, you know perfectly well I did not push the Ringmaster into that volcano," said Chuck. "I tried to stop him, but he had already become hopelessly confused by inhaling the red fumes of the Herbiscus Confusus."

"All I know is that this mission had better involve some real fighting," said Jet. "I'm itching to practice my new Australian-style moves. Who wants to see my Counter-clockwise Clonk or my Upside-down Punch?"

"I do like a meerkat who knows his moves," said a female voice.

The Clan of the Scorpion spun around, but they were unable to see where the voice had come from, until a meerkat appeared, apparently out of thin air. Bella Willowhammer landed in front of them and smiled. She wore a brimmed hat, an overcoat, and a satchel over her shoulder.

"Sissy!" exclaimed Bruce, grabbing hold of her and giving her a big hug.

"Hello, Bruce," said Bella, gasping for breath.

"Miss Willowhammer, I am pleased to meet you. I'm Chuck Cobracrusher," said Chuck, solemnly bowing.

"The name's Jet Flashfeet," said Jet, shaking her paw.

"How did you jump out of thin air like that?" demanded Donnie.

"And you must be Donnie Dragonjab," said Bella. "In answer to your question, my sudden appearance is down to this little beauty." She pressed a button on her coat collar, and a strange flying object came down from above and landed next to her. It had a circular base with a long pole in the center and propellers on top.

"Cool flying machine!" said Jet.

"Nice design," said Donnie. "But how was it invisible?"

"It wasn't," replied Bella. "The base is painted the same color as the sky. This makes it impossible to see from below, which means that it's a perfect vehicle for getting around the city unnoticed. I call it the Bella-copter."

"Bella, we are all intrigued as to why you have summoned us," said Chuck.

"I work as a private detective here in Sydney," she replied, "and I need your help. Recently I was hired by a scientist called Professor Bill Abong. He's an expert in rare plants. He sounded all jittery on the phone. He kept saying he thought he was being followed. I told him to call the police, but he'd already tried them. They laughed him out of the station."

"Why?" asked Bruce.

"He believed he was being followed by koalas."

"Koalas? You mean those cute cuddly teddy-bear things?" said Bruce.

"That cuddly stuff is just a front," said Bella. "The League of Extreme Koalas have a claw in every crime in the city."

"And were they following this scientist?" asked Chuck.

"Yes. They were watching him and I was

watching them. But they must have spotted me, because while I was keeping an eye on the professor's house late at night, they attacked me and knocked me out. When I came round, the professor had been kidnapped. So, you see, I need your help to rescue him. These koalas can be pretty rough, and I need some real fighters on my side."

"Then the Clan of the Scorpion is at your disposal," said Chuck.

"Now this sounds like a real adventure," added Jet.

CHAPTER TWO

BRUCE'S BATH OF DISCOVERY

The ninja meerkats clung on to the pole at the center of the Bella-copter while Bella flew them over the city.

"Isn't there a danger we could be seen from tall buildings?" asked Chuck, noticing that they were approaching a skyscraper.

"Don't worry about that," said Bella. She pressed a button and a screen rose up, blocking them all from view. The screen had four sets of eyeholes. While the others looked out, Donnie fiddled with his phone, tracking their progress across the city.

Bella took them over the harbor bridge, past Sydney Tower, and across town until eventually she brought the Bella-copter down on a flat rooftop. "This is where the professor lives," she explained.

The meerkats stepped off the Bella-copter. Bella pressed another button on her collar, and the flying contraption retracted until it was no larger than an umbrella.

"I was watching from that tree across the road two weeks ago when I was attacked," she continued. "I never saw my attackers, but I know it was the koalas."

"How do you know?" asked Jet.

"Because when I came to, I was sneezing like mad," she replied. "You see, I'm allergic to koala hair."

"And you believe the koalas kidnapped the professor?" said Donnie.

"No, I know the koalas were watching

him, but there is no trace of koala hair in the house. Whoever kidnapped the professor was human. Now, follow me."

She led them over the edge of the building, down a drainpipe, along a ledge, then through an open window into a carpeted hallway.

"Does anyone else know about the kidnapping?" asked Chuck.

"No one but me," replied Bella. "I've searched the house for clues, but I still don't know where they've taken him."

"With your permission we will conduct another search, in case we can discover anything more," said Chuck. "Jet, you take the bedroom. Donnie, see if you can find any information on the professor's computer. Bruce, you check the bathroom. Bella, could you talk me through the evidence you have found so far?"

Jet, Donnie, and Bruce disappeared in search of clues while Bella led Chuck down the stairs to the front door, where a coat stand lay on the ground next to a pile of shoes.

"I've pieced together the exact events of that night," said Bella. "The professor was having a bath when the doorbell rang. He got out of the bath and came downstairs in a towel, but when he opened the door, the kidnappers overcame him in a struggle. They were clearly lacking in kidnapping experience because they then led him upstairs and waited outside the bathroom while he got dressed. Once dressed, they took him back downstairs, tied his hands together, and left."

"How can you know any of this if you were unconscious?" asked Chuck.

"It's my job to know," said Bella. "When I regained consciousness, I checked the house immediately. There are no signs of forced entry, so whoever it was must have rung the doorbell. The coat stand was knocked over, which suggests a struggle.

There were still wet footprints leading down the stairs, so the professor must have been in the bath when the kidnappers arrived. Also, there are no fingerprints, so they must have been wearing gloves."

"But how do you know about the professor being led back upstairs and the kidnappers waiting outside?"

"This is a thick carpet," said Bella. "The kidnappers wore large shoes and there was one set of imprints outside the bathroom, where someone had waited while the professor dressed. That's how I know they were inexperienced kidnappers. Professionals never let the victim out of their sight, not even for a moment."

"What about tying his hands?"

"Ah, well," Bella smiled and pointed out the row of shoes by the fallen coat stand. "See how these shoes have no shoelaces?

The sleepy kidnappers must have forgotten to bring rope so they were forced to use shoelaces to tie up the professor."

"You have truly remarkable detective skills," said Chuck.

"Hey, Chuck," shouted Donnie from upstairs. "Come and check this out."

Chuck and Bella raced up the stairs to Jet and Donnie.

"What have you found?" asked Chuck.

"I hacked into the professor's computer and checked his e-mails," said Donnie. "I think I know why no one else is looking for him. In the last e-mail he sent, he says that he's off on a research trip. Here, I printed it out."

"Let me see that," said Bella, taking the e-mail and studying it carefully. "The date and time show this was written during the kidnapping, and it wasn't the professor who wrote it."

"How can you be so sure?" asked Chuck.

"Whoever wrote it spelled his name wrong. There's an extra 'g' at the end. Anyone reading it might dismiss it as a typing mistake, but I'll bet my hat one of those silly kidnappers wrote this to cover up his disappearance."

"What have you found, Jet?" asked Chuck.

"His bedroom is full of books—including the *A to Z of Rare Plants*," replied Jet. "But the volume on the letter 'H' is missing."

"Interesting, and yet we still have no clues as to where they've taken him," said Chuck.

"Where's Bruce?" asked Bella.

Suddenly, they heard a strange sound from the bathroom, as though Bruce was howling out in pain.

"Bruce is being attacked," exclaimed Jet. He leaped up and kicked the door open with a cry of "Ninja-boom!"

A cloud of steam billowed out.

"Who's there?" asked Chuck.

The steam cleared enough to reveal a blue jumpsuit lying on the floor and Bruce splashing about in a bath full of bubbles.

"Bruce, what on earth are you doing? What was that noise?" demanded Chuck.

"I couldn't find any clues in here, so I thought I'd take a bath while you were looking around. I was singing. I always sing in the bath," said Bruce.

"Oh, Bruce," said Bella, shaking her head.

"Wait a minute," said Jet. "There's something written on the mirror."

They all looked at the bathroom mirror. The steam had revealed a message. It read:

THEY'RE TAKING ME TO KOLLAWOLLABOLONG. PLEASE HELP!

"The professor must have written it when the kidnappers were waiting outside," said Donnie.

"I'll bet he overheard those half-baked kidnappers talking about it," added Bella.

"It seems as though Bruce's bath has revealed the most vital clue of all," said Chuck.

"So where is Kollawolla . . . whatever it was?" asked Jet.

"I've never heard of it," admitted Bella.

"I'll check," said Donnie. He pulled out

his phone and pressed a few buttons. "Apparently it's a dry lake about three hundred miles east of here," he said. "That's right in the Australian outback."

"Why would they take him to the outback?" said Bella. "There isn't much of anything out there."

"Whatever the reason, we must follow them," said Chuck.

"And I know just the thing to get us there," said Bella. "Come on."

THE KICKBOXING KANGAROOS
OF KOLLAWOLLABOLONG

The Indian Pacific train travels all the way across Australia, from Sydney to Perth. The train travels at an average speed of fifty-five miles per hour, and it can get pretty windy if you happen to be clinging to the top of one of the carriages, which is precisely what the five meerkats were doing.

Since there was no stop near the dry lake of Kollawollabolong, the meerkats had to use their ninja training to jump off the moving train and land safely. And judging by the way Bella hit the ground in a perfectly executed roll, it clearly wasn't the first time she had jumped from a moving train either.

However, the meerkats' ninja skills didn't help them to predict an ambush by three aggressive-looking kangaroos, wearing homemade boxing gloves.

The sudden appearance of the kangaroos didn't even give the meerkats time to dust off their fur.

"More intruders come to invade our land and disrespect our rights," said one of the kangaroos.

"Noble kangaroos, we mean you no harm," said Chuck.

All three kangaroos laughed loudly and took a step even closer.

"I'd like to see you try and harm us, mate," said the biggest kangaroo.

"Bring it on," said Jet, leaping up and spinning around, his feet coming extremely close to the kangaroo's nose. "I've got some new moves I want to practice."

"Jet, stand down," said Chuck. "Good marsupials, we are the Clan of the Scorpion."

"Yeah, well, we are the Kickboxing

Kangaroos of Kollawollabolong," replied one of the male kangaroos. "I'm Boomer, the leader of this little mob. This here is my missus, Norma, and my little brother, Jack."

The largest kangaroo flexed his muscles. "Little?" said Donnie.

Boomer chuckled. "He's a year younger, but you wouldn't believe it, would you?" Then, suddenly remembering what he was doing, he said, "Anyway, this is our land and we don't stand for trespassing."

"We are here in search of a human," said Chuck.

"So you admit you're with that rabble," said Jack. "Prepare for a pummeling. Let's get them!"

The kangaroos jumped into action and the meerkats had to dive out of the way to avoid being flattened. Boomer aimed an enormous foot at Jet, which he dodged, kicking up a cloud of dust. Jet sprang up, spun around, and whacked the kangaroo on the nose, sending him staggering back.

"You rotten flaming gallah," he exclaimed, charging back into battle.

"What's that mean?" asked Jet.

"It means I don't like you," replied Boomer.

The large kangaroo called Jack was facing Chuck and Donnie. He spun around and swung his tail at them. Chuck and Donnie leaped over it, but as they came down, Jack tried to pound them with his fists. Chuck blocked the attack with an open palm, but Jack jumped onto his back and sent Donnie flying with a powerful kick.

Bruce and Bella were busy with Norma, who was fighting as fiercely as the others. When one of Norma's punches connected with Bella, Bruce flipped out and yelled, "That's my little sister. Now you're in for some Bruce Force!"

He charged forward and knocked Norma clean off her feet.

"No one hits my ma," said a squeaky voice that came from Norma's stomach.

"Huh?" said Bruce.

Suddenly, from within Norma's pouch, appeared a fourth kangaroo. This one was much smaller than the others, but it took Bruce by surprise. It flew at him in a rage of fists and feet, with a cry of "Joey Whack Attack!"

"Now, Joey, what have I told you about scrapping?" scolded Norma, getting up and brushing herself down.

"Yes, listen to your mother. No fighting," said Boomer, while jumping around trying to flatten Jet.

"Oh, come on, it's so unfair," moaned Joey. "You all get to fight. Why can't I? Look, they're only teeny weeny."

"Only teeny weeny, eh?" said Bruce, preparing to teach the small kangaroo a lesson he wouldn't forget.

"Don't hurt him," pleaded Norma. "He's just an ankle-biter."

"He should have thought of that before taking me on," said Bruce.

"Bruce, do not harm the young one," said Chuck.

Bruce paused, giving Joey the opportunity to leap up and catch him between the eyes with his tail.

"Ow," said Bruce, rubbing his head.

"Ha, Joey Whack Attack!" proclaimed Joey.

"So you like catchphrases, do you?" asked Donnie. "Well, I've got something to catch you."

He pulled out a pistol from his backpack and fired a net that landed on top of the small kangaroo. Joey struggled to free himself, but the more he tried, the more tangled he got. Donnie pressed another button that reeled the net in, dragging the struggling kangaroo across the ground.

"Let me go," protested Joey.

"Joey!" cried Norma in distress. "Release him," she said, fixing her eyes on Donnie, in fury.

"No harm will come to him if you stop your attack," said Chuck.

"All right, you've made your point," said Boomer. "Jack, hold back."

Jack folded his arms and shuffled back to stand behind Boomer.

"Thank you," said Chuck. "As we were trying to explain, we are searching for a kidnapped human. We believe he was brought out here. You mentioned humans just now. What have you seen?"

"Well, there have been a lot of funny comings and goings. Humans, koalas, emus even. They've been around ever since Kollawollabolong vanished."

"Vanished?" asked Bella. "How can a dry lake disappear?"

"Search me. It was filled in, I suppose. We woke up one morning and it was gone. We've tried following the humans, but every time we get close, they disappear without a trace and we wind up confused."

"Don't forget about the nose," piped up Joey.

"Oh yes," said Norma, reaching into her pouch and pulling out a clown's red nose. "I found this, although none of us could remember how we got it."

"The clowns," snarled Jet, through gritted teeth.

"If they are involved, there must be a new leader," said Chuck.

"Unless they're in charge now," suggested Bruce.

"The clowns in charge. Now, that *would* be a joke," snorted Donnie.

"We've told you what we know," said Boomer. "Now release our boy."

"Let him go, Donnie," said Chuck.

Donnie released Joey from the net and he hopped back to his mother. As soon as he got near, Norma grabbed him and shoved him back into her pouch. "You're grounded for the rest of the month, young man. Do you understand?"

"But, Ma . . ." protested Joey.

"Don't 'But, Ma' me," said Norma.

"Good kangaroos," said Chuck. "We

respectfully ask your permission to follow our investigation through your land. You have my word that, as soon as we can, we will leave your territory."

"Just make sure you do," said Boomer. "Jack, Norma, let's go."

The kangaroos turned around and hopped away.

"They weren't very friendly," said Bruce.

"Their land is being invaded," said Donnie. "You can see why they were a bit jumpy, can't you!"

CHAPTER FOUR

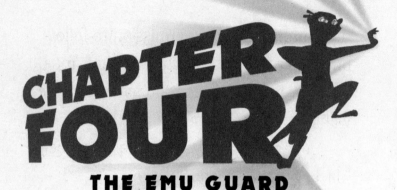

THE EMU GUARD

"I should have thought about the clowns when Bella mentioned that the kidnappers had big footprints," said Chuck.

"But what could those two want with a professor of rare plants?" asked Jet.

"Maybe they've taken up gardening," suggested Bruce.

"Not likely. They're a pair of weeds themselves," said Donnie.

"The question is, how are we going to find them?" asked Bruce.

"I've got an idea," said Bella. She pulled

out a large magnifying glass from her bag and dropped to her knees. "The kangaroos said there had been lots of people coming and going. Let's see if they left any clues."

"Ooh, a magnifying glass! That reminds me, I'm starving," said Bruce.

"How does a magnifying glass remind you of that?" asked Jet.

"It's a great way of cooking ants," Bruce replied simply.

Bella took a close look through the magnifying glass. "There's a tire mark."

The others gathered around to see.

"It's pretty faint, but it's there all right."

"So whoever took the professor came in a car," said Jet.

"Except there's only one tire mark," said Bella.

"Perhaps it was a wheelbarrow," suggested Donnie.

"Or a unicycle," said Chuck.

"A unicycle," said Jet. "Hey, remember that hypnotist we met when we fought the Ringmaster in America? He was on a unicycle. What was his name?"

"Hans Free," said Donnie. "Perhaps he's in charge now. Where does the track lead?"

"It's been blown away by the wind," said Bella, looking down again. "But look." She picked up a hair and sniffed it. "Ah— ah— chooo!" she sneezed.

"Bless you," said Chuck.

"Koalas," she muttered, dropping on to all fours and sniffing until she sneezed again.

"What are you doing, sis?" asked Bruce.

"She's sniffing out the route the koalas took," replied Chuck.

They watched as Bella moved on to the next hair.

"Her skills of detection are certainly nothing to sniff at," said Donnie.

The meerkats followed Bella across the dry landscape under the blazing sun. After almost an hour and countless sneezes, they spotted a large rock. Next to it was an emu, marching back and forward.

"It looks as though that emu's guarding something," said Chuck, dodging behind a rock to avoid being spotted. The others crouched down beside him.

"Guarding what?" asked Bruce. "All I

can see is that rock."

"Let's go and find out," said Jet eagerly. He went to move into the open, but Chuck blocked his way.

"No, we must be subtle before we are bold."

"Then I have just the thing," said Donnie. From his bag he pulled out a large feathery costume. "When I heard we were going to Australia, I took the precaution of dusting off the old emu disguise," he said.

"Good work, Donnie," said Chuck.

Behind the rock, the meerkats assembled the disguise and climbed inside. Donnie gave the job of operating the two stilt-legs to Jet and Bruce, while he held up the long pole with the head on top. Chuck and Bella balanced on Jet and Bruce's shoulders and watched where they were going using eyeholes in the bird's stomach. After hitching the bird disguise up onto its two legs, they made their way unsteadily toward the emu.

"Do you think this is better than simply approaching undisguised?" whispered Bella.

"We would prefer it if our enemies did not know of our presence," said Chuck. "Now please allow me to do the talking. If the emu is to believe the disguise, it must only hear one voice."

"Halt. Who goes there? Friend or foe?" said the emu, turning around to confront them.

"Oh, I'm sorry, I'm a bit lost," replied Chuck, operating a lever that made the beak move in time with his words. "I'm looking for Kollawolla. . . ."

"Kollawollabolong," said the emu haughtily. "Well, I can't help you. It's a classified secret that this is the spot where the dry lake was—before it was covered over."

"And I can see that you're busy guarding this very important rock," replied Chuck.

"That's right, so I'll have to ask you to move along, please," said the emu.

"I've never known a rock that needed guarding before."

"This is no ordinary rock," said the emu, lowering his voice. "I couldn't tell you what it is though. It's a classified secret."

"And I wouldn't dream of asking," said Chuck.

"Good. Because it's my job to stop any sticky beaks discovering that this rock is, in fact, a secret entrance to a secret lab built secretly inside the old dry lake," said the emu proudly.

"You're doing a splendid job of keeping it a secret," said Chuck. "I imagine it's got a really clever way of opening, too."

"That's right," the emu nodded. "You

see this here?" He pointed to a hollow tree trunk sticking out of the ground.

"Yes," said Chuck.

"It's what we call a didgeridoo," whispered the emu. "Authorized personnel wanting to enter just have to blow into it to open the secret entrance to the secret lab. Anyway, you'd better be off now. I have important guard duties to fulfil."

From somewhere inside the emu, another voice spoke. "Is it time to be bold now?"

"Yes, Jet, I'd say a roundhouse kick should do it," replied Chuck.

"What did you say?" asked the emu.

At that moment, Jet brought the stilt-leg he was manoeuvring swinging around and kicked the emu. It toppled over, out cold.

The force of the move and the fact that there was only one leg left holding it up meant that the emu disguise toppled over and sent the meerkats crashing to the ground.

"Oh, very subtle," said Bella, crawling out.

"We extracted the information we needed without revealing our identities," said Chuck, while Donnie packed the disguise away. "When he comes around, he'll say he was attacked by another emu. That's subtle enough. Now we must get inside."

"Leave it to me," said Jet. He scampered up the didgeridoo, pushed his whole head inside, and gave a big blow, creating a long deep note that caused the ground to vibrate.

"You know how to play the didgeridoo!" said Bella, clearly impressed. "You must have been to Australia before."

"No, but the circular breathing we use in our martial-arts training is the same that is required to play the didgeridoo," replied Jet.

In response to the sound, part of the rock slid slowly to the side, revealing a dark tunnel leading underground.

"They must be up to something serious for all this secrecy and security," remarked Donnie.

"Look," said Bella. "There's the tire track again—it goes straight in." She was down on all fours to look at it when suddenly she sneezed. The sound echoed around the tunnel walls.

"Sorry," she said.

"I think you'd better have this," said Donnie, reaching into his bag and pulling out a piece of white material.

"I've got a hanky, thanks," said Bella.

"This is no hanky," replied Donnie. "It's an air-filtering mask. It protects your nose from the koala hair and stops you sneezing."

"Good work, Donnie," said Chuck. "Bella's nose has proved useful getting us this far, but a sneeze now could end up blowing it for all of us."

CHAPTER FIVE

FAMILIAR FACES AND FEARSOME FOES

The five meerkats entered the tunnel and the rock slid back into place behind them. Donnie pulled out a head torch from his gadget bag and switched it on.

"It's very peculiar that this could all have been made without the kangaroos knowing about it," said Bella.

"They said that each time they followed the intruders, they ended up confused," said Chuck thoughtfully.

"Maybe the clowns have found some way of confusing people," said Donnie.

"Like the plant on Dragon Island—
Herbiscus Confusus?" suggested Jet.

"It can't be," said Donnie. "We stopped
the Ringmaster and his cronies from stealing
it and chased them off Dragon Island."

"True," said Jet. "But it would explain
why the volume on the letter 'H' was
missing from the *A to Z of Rare Plants*."

"We are certainly getting closer to
solving the mystery. We must proceed with
caution—the red smoke of the Herbiscus
Confusus was very powerful," said Chuck.
"Donnie, do you have more masks?"

"Sorry, that's the only one," admitted
Donnie.

"Then we have even more reason to be
cautious," said Chuck. "Remember, our goal
is to find Professor Abong."

When they reached a point where the
tunnel divided in two, the meerkats stopped.

"Donnie, Bruce, and Bella, take the right tunnel," said Chuck. "Jet and I will take the left."

"Here, take my flashlight," said Bella, handing him one from inside her coat.

"Thank you," said Chuck. "And like the elephant who tiptoes across the minefield, we must tread carefully."

With these parting words, Chuck and Jet headed along the left-hand passageway. They walked in silence until they came to another junction.

"Someone's coming," said Jet.

Chuck turned off the light and they ducked out of sight.

"Hold it carefully now, Greggles, mate," said a voice. "We don't want to breathe in this stuff, especially since you went and lost our masks."

"I *am* holding it carefully, Robbo. Besides, I didn't lose them. I put them in the wash. It's disgusting, having to wear them all day long and never washing them."

Two koalas appeared around the corner, both wearing head flashlights and carrying a large bucket between them. Jet peered out, but he couldn't see what was inside the bucket as there was a lid on top.

"I've had it with all this lugging," said Greggles. "I didn't join the League of Extreme Koalas to lug buckets around."

"Yeah, but it's not long now till everything's ready," said Robbo. "Then there'll be no more lugging for us. We'll be giving orders and the rest of the world will be following them."

Greggles put down his side of the bucket. "Funny sort of plan in my opinion, mate. If you ask me, these fruit loops we're working with ain't all there. They're two corks short of a whole hat, if you know what I mean. They're one shrimp short of a full barbie. They're as crazy as a dingo with its tail on fire." He slammed his fist down on the bucket. The lid flew up and a wisp of red smoke came drifting out.

"What are you playing at?" snapped Robbo, pushing the lid back into place.

Greggles looked blankly at the other koala. "Hey, what's going on? What's this bucket for?" he said.

"You've inhaled the fumes, you fool," said Robbo.

"I've what the what? Hey, why have we got these lights on our heads? Where are we?"

"Pick up your side of the bucket and come on," ordered Robbo.

Greggles looked confused, but he did as he was told. They carried on through the tunnel and around the corner.

Jet and Chuck emerged from the shadows and followed them.

"Did you see that red smoke?" said Jet. "It was just like the smoke on Dragon Island from the Herbiscus Confusus."

"Aye, and there's a good reason for that," said a voice behind them.

Chuck and Jet spun around, but all they saw was a cloud of red smoke billowing toward them.

In the other tunnel, Donnie, Bruce, and Bella had spotted a light up ahead.

Donnie switched off his flashlight and they approached cautiously. The tunnel led into a vast cave. The meerkats crept inside and hid behind a stack of buckets to take in the incredible scene. The cave was filled with shiny equipment and strange machinery. In the center were twenty huge missiles, pointing up at the ceiling. To the side of the missiles, there was an elevated area with consoles displaying rows of buttons, levers, and screens.

"It's a missile base," said Donnie.

"Missiles?" exclaimed Bella.

"No ordinary missiles either," said Donnie. "Look at those koalas over there."

There were dozens of koalas wearing white masks over their mouths and carrying buckets back and forth from a huge vat in one corner of the room. Every time the vat was opened, a wispy red gas escaped from inside.

"I recognize that gas," said Donnie. "It's made when the Herbiscus Confusus is burned. They must be filling these missiles with the red smoke so that they can cause massive explosions of confusion."

"Wouldn't they just hit the ceiling if they went off?" asked Bruce.

"No. Look closer. There's a gap down the middle so the roof can be slid back when the missiles are launched," said Donnie.

"And look, there's the professor! We've found him!" said Bella.

At the far side of the cave, surrounded by bubbling test tubes was Professor Abong.

"He's helping them!" said Bruce.

"I think I can see why," said Donnie. He pointed out a man on a unicycle, dangling a watch on a chain in front of the professor. "Hans Free, the unicycling hypnotist, is controlling the professor. They must have needed his expertise to use the plant smoke as a weapon."

"How can we get him out of his trance?" asked Bella.

"A sharp slap to the face should do it," replied Donnie.

"I can see some other people in need of a few slaps," said Bruce. "Look up there—it's the Von Trapeze family." The seven evil siblings were hanging from high wires.

"Who's that with the knives?" asked Bella.

"His name is Herr Flick," said Donnie.

"And like the rest of them, he'll be experiencing some Bruce Force soon enough," snarled Bruce, clenching his fists.

"Hang on," said Donnie, holding him back. "Here come the clowns."

Grimsby and Sheffield entered the cave. Grimsby was carrying a bucket, while Sheffield held a large gun. Like everyone else, both wore white masks.

"Hold up," said Grimsby. "There's a hole in my bucket."

"What kind of hole, Grimsby?"

"A *whole* meerkat," said Grimsby. He tipped the bucket over and Chuck and Jet fell out. The clowns laughed.

"Actually, that's two whole meerkats," said Sheffield.

"What's going on?" asked Chuck.

"I'm sure there was something we were supposed to be doing," said Jet.

"Feeling confused?" said Sheffield, pulling the trigger on his gun and sending a cloud of red smoke into their faces.

When it cleared, Jet and Chuck looked at each other with puzzled expressions.

"Excellent work," said a deep voice.

Donnie and Bruce looked at each other. They couldn't see the speaker from their hiding place behind the buckets, but they recognized the voice.

"But that sounds like—" started Bruce.

"It can't be!" said Donnie.

"Who?" asked Bella.

A man stepped into the cave. He was a shadowy figure wearing a tall hat and holding a whip in one hand. He walked with a slight limp and wore a black mask, but his identity was unmistakable.

"The Ringmaster," gasped Donnie and Bruce together.

CHAPTER SIX

EVIL EXPLANATIONS

Even in his dazed state of mind, Chuck could sense that there was something familiar about the man standing in front of him wearing a top hat. "It's to do with rings," said Chuck, trying to uncloud his mind. "Ring-mapper? Ring-monster?"

The masked clown went to fire his strange-looking gun again, but the Ringmaster stopped him. "No," he said. "I want them to fully understand what I'm going to tell them. Don't worry, Herr Flick will skewer them if either one moves."

A tall blond man wearing a red shirt and a black waistcoat drew two knives from his belt and aimed them at Chuck and Jet. "*Ja, mein Ringmaster.* It will be a pleasure to finally skewer these two meddlesome *meerkatzchen.*"

"Ringmaster?" said Chuck vaguely.

"Struggling to make sense of it all?" said the Ringmaster. "Don't worry. The smoke in these guns is a less potent version of the confusion smoke. The effects won't last long."

"I know you," said Chuck.

"Yes, when you last saw me, I was plummeting down into a volcano on Dragon Island."

"Dragon Island," said Jet vaguely. "The Ultimate Dragon Warrior."

"When you sent my balloon into the volcano, you thought you had prevented me from stealing the Herbiscus Confusus," said the Ringmaster.

"The red-flowered plant," said Chuck.

"But my balloon got caught halfway down the volcano," continued the Ringmaster. "I would have remained there in a state of confusion had my faithful Doris not risked the volcano to come to my rescue."

Doris, the Ringmaster's dancing dog, rubbed herself against his shins, revealing her patchy white fur, where the volcano had burned her.

The Ringmaster tickled her chin. "She was brave enough to come after me when the rest of my troupe ran away like cowards."

"We didn't run away, boss," said Grimsby.

"Yeah, it was more like advancing backwards," said Sheffield.

The Ringmaster cracked his whip angrily at the clown. "Thankfully Doris knows the true meaning of loyalty. She had cleverly stolen one of the lemur's masks so she was unaffected by the smoke. It took several days, but slowly Doris dragged me to safety.

By the time we reached the top, the lemurs who protect the precious plant had gone, assuming, like you, that we had perished."

"You escaped," said Chuck.

"When I came to my senses," said the Ringmaster, "I instantly realized what an opportunity I had. Doris went back into the volcano and retrieved as many flowers from the Herbiscus Confusus as she could carry. Once we had these, all we needed was an expert in rare plants to help us extract the essence and create weapons. Professor Abong was the perfect man for the job—he just needed a little persuasion."

The Ringmaster pointed to the professor. Chuck and Jet looked over to where Professor Abong was working. Hans Free cycled around him, swinging his watch.

"And we enlisted the League of Extreme

Koalas to create this base."

"But as usual you failed to take into account that the Clan of the Scorpion will always be there to stop you," said Chuck, now fully recovered from the effect of the smoke.

The Ringmaster threw his head back and laughed. "Ah, yes, the Clan of the Scorpion. Four deadly ninja meerkats dedicated to stopping me. And yet, there are only two of you, which means the other two are hidden somewhere nearby, listening to all this." The Ringmaster cracked his whip so that the sound echoed around the chamber. "Donnie, Bruce," he called. "Come out, come out, wherever you are."

Neither showed themselves.

"Very well. I will count to three, then you will appear with your paws held high

or else Herr Flick will turn Chuck and Jet
into meer-kebabs. One . . . Two . . ."
Herr Flick took aim.

"Stop!"

Donnie and Bruce stepped out from their hiding place.

"Oh, so predictable," said the Ringmaster with a smile.

"You won't get away with this," said Bruce.

"You never were the sharpest tool in the box, were you, Willowhammer?" said the Ringmaster. "Otherwise you'd see that getting away with this is exactly what I'm about to do. Soon I will fire these missiles. They are programmed to target every major city in the world. . . . London, Tokyo, New York. The confusion smoke within these missiles is so strong that it will take weeks for the effects to wear off. Once everyone is lost in confusion, my circus troupe will move in and take power quicker than you can say, 'The Clan of the Scorpion have been defeated.'"

"Not while there's any breath left in our bodies, you won't," said Donnie.

"Which won't be very long," said the Ringmaster. "Now, be a good ninja and throw your gadget bag away—or Herr Flick will make sure Chuck gets the point."

"No, Donnie! Don't!" said Chuck.

"Sorry, Chuck," said Donnie. He threw his bag to the side. It landed by the buckets.

The Von Trapeze family swung closer to them, prepared to attack.

"Hey, Grimsby, knock knock," said Sheffield.

"Who's there?" replied Grimsby.

"Luke."

"Luke who?"

"*Looks* like we've actually won this time!" Sheffield guffawed.

"And now it's my turn to tell a joke," said the Ringmaster with a triumphant laugh. "The one about the man who destroyed his sworn enemies and took over the world."

This time the Ringmaster's laughter was joined by the cackles of his goons, Doris's barks, and the applause from the koalas, who waved their confusion guns in the air.

CHAPTER SEVEN

THE FIFTH MEERKAT

"Shall I finish them off, *mein Ringmaster?*" asked Herr Flick.

"No," said the Ringmaster. "I would like them all to witness the moment when I finally take control of the world. Hey, you two." He pointed at Robbo and Greggles, the two koalas Chuck and Jet had overheard in the tunnel. "It's time to open the roof so that these missiles can be fired."

"I didn't join the League of Extreme Koalas to open roofs," grumbled Greggles.

"How dare you answer me back!" exclaimed the Ringmaster.

"He didn't mean anything by it," said Robbo quickly. Out of the side of his mouth he said, "Be quiet, Greggles. Just do as he says."

The two koalas clambered up onto a console and pressed a few buttons. Slowly the roof of the laboratory slid back, revealing the clear blue sky overhead.

"You see," said the Ringmaster, "this is not only a weapons factory. It is also a launch pad for these missiles."

The Ringmaster picked up a
microphone and his booming voice filled
the cave. "Ladies and gentlemen, boys and
girls . . . circus goons and koalas," he cried.
"Soon the world will bow down before us.
Any who stand in our way will be thrown
into confusion. The entire world will be one
big circus and I will be its all-powerful
Ringmaster!"

He cracked his whip and, once again,
the army of koalas and circus goons
dutifully applauded.

"Not so fast, Ringmaster," said Chuck.
"Before the Clan each enemy cowers, for
now we fight till victory is ours!"

"Ha," scoffed the Ringmaster. "Even if
you avoided Herr Flick's knives, none of you
have masks. You are in my power!"

"But I'm not!" said a voice.

The Ringmaster turned and saw a

female meerkat wearing a wide-brimmed hat, and holding two bags. Bella Willowhammer drew a pistol from Donnie's bag and fired a net that flew into the air and came down on Herr Flick.

As the knife thrower struggled to get free, the meerkats leaped into action, each of them tearing a mask off an unsuspecting koala and putting it on to protect themselves from the confusion smoke.

"Ringmaster, meet Bella Willowhammer," said Chuck. "And prepare to face defeat."

Chuck drew his sword and sliced through the barrel of a gun that one of the koalas was pointing at him, causing red gas to pour from the broken end. He then expertly sliced off the koala's mask, forcing

him to breathe in the smoke.

Jet jumped high into the air and performed three backward somersaults over the heads of several rows of koalas before coming down head first and executing a series of perfectly aimed powerful punches, sending koalas flying.

"How do you like my Upside-down Attack?" he cried. "Ninja-boom!"

The other meerkats were also busy taking advantage of the confusion.

Bella threw Donnie's backpack to him. "Thanks," he said, putting it on.

Ten angry koalas charged at him, but he pulled out two handfuls of marbles and sent them across the floor, causing the koalas to lose their footing and slide into each other.

With a cry of "Bruce Force!" Bruce charged at the clowns, knocking them off their feet and kicking their weapons from their hands.

"Get those ninjas," cried the Ringmaster furiously.

While every koala and circus goon charged at the Clan of the Scorpion, Bella pulled her Bella-copter from her bag, unfolded it, and used it to fly over to the professor.

"Professor Abong," she said, bringing the Bella-copter level with his face.

He stared at her blankly.

"Sorry about this," she said and she gave him a sharp slap around the face.

"Good grief. What is going on?" he asked. "What is this place? And why does my face hurt so much?"

"I'm Bella Willowhammer. You hired me to find out who was following you. You've been hypnotized into helping a band of criminals intent on taking over the world. I'm here to rescue you!"

"I do not think so," said Hans Free, swinging his watch in front of her eyes.

"Look into my eyes, my dear."

Jet saw what was happening and rushed toward Hans Free. "Oh no, you don't," he cried, leaping up into the air then coming down in a super-fast spin and knocking Hans Free's watch out of his hands.

"That was the Counter-clockwise Clonk," said Jet. "Moob-ajnin! That's 'Ninja-boom' backwards!"

Disoriented by the blow, Hans Free's unicycle spun out of control and sent him careering into a row of koalas.

"This meerkat mayhem will not prevent the missiles from launching," shouted the Ringmaster. "Koalas, hit the ignition button."

"I didn't join the League of Extreme Koalas to hit buttons," grumbled Greggles.

"Oh, shush," said Robbo. He pushed a large red button on the console.

Suddenly, the missiles that stood in the center of the base began to rumble. With an ear-shattering *BOOM* and a burst of flame and smoke, they launched into the sky, flying toward the targeted cities.

"At last," yelled the Ringmaster. "The world is mine!"

CHAPTER EIGHT

A GREAT ESCAPE

The missiles soared into the sky, leaving thick white vapor trails behind them. In the base below, the battle continued. Jet was surrounded by koalas, who were taking turns to charge at him. They were surprisingly acrobatic, performing midair somersaults before coming crashing down to attack with their claws and fists, but they were no match for Jet's skills. Koalas went flying as he launched himself at them, spinning with his arms outstretched, chopping through them like a lawnmower through grass.

Not far from him, Bella and Bruce were
working together, while Professor Abong
cowered in a corner, wearing the mask
Bella had snatched off Hans Free. Bella had
gotten hold of a large smoke gun and was
firing the confusion smoke at yet more

koalas, while Bruce ran through their ranks, tearing off their masks. As soon as they breathed in the red gas, they stopped fighting and stood looking puzzled, until Bruce bowled them over like bowling pins.

With the roof open, a strong breeze blew through the base, sending the gas in all directions. Everyone without a mask was affected by the confusion.

"Donnie, we have to stop the missiles," called Chuck, who was slicing masks off the Von Trapeze family with his sword.

Donnie grabbed a gas-gun from a koala and fired it at the evil siblings. "I agree," he said. "But we'll need to get past the Ringmaster first."

The Ringmaster stood in front of the control panel, with Doris beside him. She growled threateningly.

"I should be able to override the target of the missiles if I can get to that panel," said Donnie.

"Leave it to me," said Chuck. With his sword drawn, he approached the Ringmaster.

"Ah, Chuck Cobracrusher," said the Ringmaster, cracking his whip. "Will I never see the end of you?"

"Like a boomerang, I just keep coming back," snarled Chuck.

"Not for much longer! Do you know what they call a boomerang that doesn't come back? A stick," replied the villain, turning to his dog. "And I know someone who likes fetching sticks. Doris!"

Doris leaped into the air and landed into a head spin, kicking her legs around viciously. Chuck stepped back to avoid being hit. He was about to kick her off balance when something landed heavily on the console with a cry of "Joey Whack Attack!"

Three more crashes indicated the arrival of the other kangaroos, jumping through the open roof into the base.

"G'day! We couldn't help but notice Kollawollabolong suddenly reappear," said Boomer. "They'd covered over the lake!"

"And we saw the missiles launch," said Jack.

"So we thought you might be in need of some help," said Norma.

"And I'm no longer grounded," exclaimed Joey, jumping up and pummeling the Ringmaster's face.

Doris tried to defend the Ringmaster, but Norma dealt her a forceful kick. "You stay away from my Joey, you no-good mutt," she warned.

"Circus goons," cried the Ringmaster, trying to bat Joey away. "Get these kangaroos."

Sheffield and Grimsby came charging at Joey, but Jack, Boomer, and Norma were working as a team and kicked the confusion guns out of their hands before they had a chance to fire them. Chuck threw masks to the kangaroos so they wouldn't be affected by the confusion smoke. They fought the circus goons and koalas with a torrent of swinging tails, thumping feet, and pounding fists.

Chuck joined Donnie under the console. "Quickly, Donnie," he yelled. "The missiles!"

Donnie climbed on top of the console and looked with dismay at the rows of buttons that had been broken or crushed by the impact of the kangaroos' huge feet. He quickly set about twiddling knobs and

pulling levers.

Chuck looked for the Ringmaster, only
to see that he and Doris had fled to the far
corner of the laboratory. They were inflating
a black-and-red hot-air balloon. Chuck was
about to give chase when Donnie shouted,
"Chuck, Jet, Bella, Bruce! Over here!"

The others fought their way over to Donnie.

"What is it?" asked Jet. "I was just getting warmed up."

"Good news and bad news," said Donnie. "The good news is that I've found a way to redirect the missiles to an alternative target, saving the world from the Ringmaster's evil plan. The bad news is that since the kangaroos broke the controls, there is only one place I could redirect the missiles to, and that's back here."

"Back here?" exclaimed the other four meerkats.

"Back here," repeated Donnie. "In a minute there's going to be a massive confusion explosion. We need to evacuate the cave."

Chuck grabbed a microphone from the

mission control console and turned it on.

"Attention, everyone." Chuck's amplified voice echoed around the base. "The missiles are heading back to Kollawollabolong. Unless you want to be extremely confused, you need to get out now."

Chuck had barely finished his sentence when the circus goons and hundreds of koalas stopped attacking, turned tail, and ran. Those who were too confused to understand were grabbed by the ones with masks and dragged away. They climbed up the scaffolding of the Von Trapeze family's high wires and pushed bits of equipment against the walls, enabling them to scramble up and out.

"Hold up, make way now," said Sheffield.

"I didn't join the League of Extreme Koalas to get out of your way," grumbled Greggles.

"Yeah! Off you run from my incredible Joey Whack Attack!" exclaimed Joey, punching the air.

"You kangaroos had better get going too," said Chuck. "Can you take care of the professor? We need to get him out of here! You'll have to move fast though. There isn't much time before impact."

"Sure thing," said Boomer. "Climb on."

"A lift from a kangaroo. How confusing," muttered the professor.

"Things are going to get a lot more confusing if you don't get going," said Chuck.

The professor climbed onto Jack's back, while Norma bundled Joey into her pouch, in spite of his protests that he was perfectly capable of jumping out himself. The kangaroos then leaped up onto the console, from where they could jump out of the base.

The roaring noise above grew louder and louder. The meerkats looked up to see the missiles hurtling toward them.

"What's the plan, Donnie?" asked Jet.

"It involves the Bella-copter and one of those missile boosters," replied Donnie.

A great red mushroom cloud went up as the missiles collided with the Ringmaster's secret base. At the top of the rising cloud were five meerkats, clinging on to the central pole of a small propeller-operated flying machine, with a huge rocket booster hastily attached to the bottom.

"What an explosion," shouted Jet. "Ninja-BAH-BOOM!"

"Do you think the kangaroos got away in time?" asked Bella, looking down at the massive cloud beneath them.

"Look! They're over there," said Donnie.

The kangaroos were hopping at an incredible speed, staying just ahead of the expanding cloud of smoke.

"I don't think the koalas are quite as fast," said Bruce.

"Yes, there'll be a cluster of confused koalas kicking around in Kollawollabolong for some time," said Chuck.

"Try saying that with a mouth full of marshmallows," said Donnie.

"But perhaps when they come to their senses, they will have forgotten about the League of Extreme Koalas altogether," Chuck added.

"What about the Ringmaster?" asked Bella.

"He's managed to get away, too. Look!" said Jet. They could see the black-and-red hot-air balloon floating away.

"No matter where he goes, he should know we will be right behind him—ready to thwart his next evil scheme," said Chuck.

"At least he won't be able to use the Herbiscus Confusus again," said Donnie. "That weapons factory has been well and truly destroyed by the missiles."

For a moment, the meerkats looked down in silence, then Bruce said, "That reminds me, we haven't eaten for ages! I'm starving."

"What about this situation could possibly remind you of food?" asked Chuck.

"Well, it's a mushroom cloud, isn't it!" replied Bruce. "Mushrooms. Yum!"

Go Fish!

GOFISH

Gareth P. Jones

What did you want to be when you grew up?
At various points, a writer, a musician, an intergalactic bounty hunter and, for a limited period, a graphic designer. (I didn't know what that meant, but I liked the way it sounded.)

When did you realize you wanted to be a writer?
I don't remember realizing it. I have always loved stories. From a very young age, I enjoyed making them up. As I'm not very good at making things up on the spot, this invariably involved having to write them down.

What's an embarrassing childhood memory?
Seriously? There are too many. I have spent my entire life saying and doing embarrassing things. Just thinking about some of them is making me cringe. Luckily, I have a terrible memory, so I can't remember them all, but no, I'm not going to write any down for you. If I did that, I'd never be able to forget them.

What's your favorite childhood memory?
To be honest with you, I don't remember my childhood very well at all (I told you I had a bad memory), but I do recall how my dad used to tell me stories. He would make them up as he went along, most likely borrowing all sorts of elements from the books he was reading without me knowing.

As a young person, who did you look up to most?
My mom and dad, Prince, Michael Jackson, all of Monty Python, and Stephen Fry.

What was your favorite thing about school?
Laughing with my friends.

What was your least favorite thing about school?
I had a bit of a hard time when I moved from the Midlands to London at the age of twelve because I had a funny accent. But don't worry, it was all right in the end.

What were your hobbies as a kid? What are your hobbies now?
I love listening to and making music. My hobbies haven't really changed over the years, except that there's a longer list of instruments now. When I get a chance, I like idling away the day playing trumpet, guitar, banjo, ukulele, mandolin (and piano if there's one in the vicinity). I also like playing out with my friends.

What was your first job, and what was your "worst" job?

My first job was working as a waiter. That's probably my worst job, too. As my dad says, I was a remarkably grumpy waiter. I'm not big on all that serving-people malarkey.

What book is on your nightstand now?

I have a pile of books from my new publisher. I'm trying to get through them before I meet the authors. I'm half-way through *Maggot Moon* by Sally Gardner, which is written in the amazing voice of a dyslexic boy.

How did you celebrate publishing your first book?

The first time I saw one of my books in a shop, I was so excited that I caused something of a commotion. I managed to persuade an unsuspecting customer to buy it so I could sign it for her son.

Where do you write your books?

Anywhere and everywhere. Here are some of the locations I have written the Ninja Meerkats series: On the 185 and the 176 buses in London, various airplanes, Hong Kong, Melbourne, all over New Zealand, a number of cafes and bars between San Diego and San Francisco, New Quay in South Wales, and my kitchen.

What sparked your imagination for the Ninja Meerkats?

The idea came from the publishing house, but from the moment I heard it, I really wanted to write it. It reminded me of lots of action-packed cartoons I used to watch when I was young. I love the fact that I get to cram in lots of jokes and puns, fast action, and crazy outlandish plots.

The Ninja Meerkats are awesome fighters; have you ever studied martial arts? If so, what types?
Ha, no. If I was to get into a fight, my tactic would be to fall over and hope that whoever was attacking me lost interest.

If you were a Ninja Meerkat, what would your name be?
Hmm, how about Gareth *POW!* Jones?

What's your favorite exhibit or animal at the zoo?
Funnily enough, I like the meerkats. I was at a zoo watching them the other day when it started to rain. They suddenly ran for cover, looking exactly like their human visitors.

What's Bruce's favorite food?
Anything with the words ALL YOU CAN EAT written above it.

If you had a catchphrase like Bruce Force! or Ninja-Boom! what would it be?
That's a tricky one. How about PEN POWER!

If you were a Ninja Meerkat, what would your special ninja skill be?
I like to think I'd be like Jet, and always working on a new skill. When I got into school, I took the Random Move

Generator! We used it to come up with new moves, like the Floating Butterfly Punch and the Ultimate Lemon Punch.

What is your favorite thing about real-life meerkats? Have you ever met a meerkat?
I was lucky enough to go into a meerkat enclosure recently. They were crawling all over me, trying to get a good view. It was brilliant.

What challenges do you face in the writing process, and how do you overcome them?
The challenge with writing the Ninja Meerkats books is mostly about the plotting. It's trying to get all the twists and turns to work, and to avoid them feeling predictable. When I hit problems, I write down as many options as I can think of from the completely ordinary to utterly ridiculous. Once they're all down on paper, the right answer normally jumps out at me.

Which of your characters is most like you?
I'd like to say that I'm wise and noble like Chuck, but I'm probably more like the Ringmaster as we're both always coming up with new ways to take over the world.

What makes you laugh out loud?
My friends.

What do you do on a rainy day?
Play guitar, write, watch TV, or go out with my sword-handled umbrella.

What's your idea of fun?
Answering questionnaires about myself. Actually, tomorrow, I'm going to a music festival with my wife where we will dance and cavort. That should be fun.

What's your favorite song?
There are far too many to mention, but today I think I'll go for "Feel Good Inc." by Gorillaz.

Who is your favorite fictional character?
Another tricky one, but today I'll say Ged from the Earthsea Trilogy by Ursula K. Le Guin.

What was your favorite book when you were a kid?
As a child, I especially loved *The Phantom Tollbooth* by Norton Juster.

What's your favorite TV show or movie?
Raiders of the Lost Ark.

If you were stranded on a desert island, who would you want for company?
My wife and son, then probably my friend Pete, as he's really handy and would be able to make and build things.

If you could travel anywhere in the world, where would you go and what would you do?
I'd like to go to Canada next. Ideally, I'd like to go and live there for a bit. I've never been to South America. There are also lots of parts of America I haven't visited yet.

If you could travel in time, where would you go and what would you do?
I think I'd travel to the future and see what's changed and whether anyone's invented a new kind of umbrella.

What's the best advice you have ever received about writing?
Don't tell the story, show the story.

What advice do you wish someone had given you when you were younger?
Everything's probably going to be fine, so it's best to enjoy yourself.

Do you ever get writer's block? What do you do to get back on track?
It feels like tempting fate, but I don't really believe in writer's block. I think if you can't write, you're doing the wrong thing. You may need to plan or jot down options or go for a walk.

What do you want readers to remember about your books?
I'd settle for a general feeling of having enjoyed them.

What would you do if you ever stopped writing?
I'd do a full stop. If this is for an American audience, I guess that would be a period.

What should people know about you?
I'm a very silly man.

What do you like best about yourself?
I'm a very silly man.

Do you have any strange or funny habits? Did you when you were a kid?
I talk to myself a lot, which is probably pretty common, but the difference is that I don't listen to what I'm saying.

CHUCK
COBRACRUSHER

Leader of the Clan
(and the brains)

Specialist ninja skill:
Nifty with the sword

Most likely to be heard saying:
Before the Clan, each enemy cowers,
for now we fight till victory is ours!

Most likely to be found:
Meditating or practicing his swordplay
(though not at the same time)

Famous for:
Remaining calm under pressure

SMALL. GRIPPY. DEADLY.

NINJA
MEERKATS

JET
FLASHFEET

Super fast ninja
A lean, mean fighting machine

Specialist ninja skill:
A dab hand with the nunchucks
Most likely to be heard saying:
Ninja-boom!
Most likely to be found:
Practicing his moves and reading his
collection of magazines and books.
His favorites are *What Karate!*,
101 More Martial Arts Moves
and *Kung Fu Weekly*
Famous for:
His impetuous ways, which
can lead to trouble . . .

SMALL. FURRY. DEADLY.

NINJA MEERKATS

BRUCE
WILLOWHAMMER

aka Bruce "the muscle" Willowhammer
The clue's in the name, this fella is a mighty powerhouse of strength

Specialist ninja skill:
The throw — anytime, any place, anywhere . . . anyone . . .

Most likely to be heard saying:
Time for some Bruce Force!

Most likely to be found:
Doing 100 press-ups while planning a BIG breakfast

Famous for:
His bottomless appetite

NINJA MEERKATS

DONNIE
DRAGONJAB

Brilliant inventor
and master of gadgets

Specialist ninja skill:
Being able to turn anything into
a deadly weapon
Most likely to be heard saying:
Something sarcastic
Most likely to be found:
Taking things apart, putting things
back together, and devising cunning
disguises
Famous for:
His love of technology

SMALL. FURRY. DEADLY.

NINJA MEERKATS